This book belongs to
_____

This book is dedicated to my children - Mikey, Kobe, and Jojo.

Copyright © 2024 Grow Grit Press LLC. All rights reserved. No part of this book may be reproduced in any form without permission in writing from the publisher. Please send bulk order requests to info@ninjalifehacks.tv

Paperback ISBN: 978-1-63731-875-1
Hardcover ISBN: 978-1-63731-877-5
eBook ISBN: 978-1-63731-876-8

Printed and bound in the USA.
NinjaLifeHacks.tv

Ninja Life Hacks®
by Mary Nhin

Visionary Ninja

A Children's Book About Seeing What Others Can't

Ninja Life Hacks®
by Mary Nhin

A - Then, I started to **ASSEMBLE**! I put the pieces together like a puzzle. Some were big, some small, but I didn't give up. I kept going.

Days turned into weeks, and my spaceship started taking shape. But something was missing. It needed a special touch.

I remembered what my grandpa always said,

Visionaries think differently. They see what others can't.

My spaceship was finally complete! It looked amazing with its shiny parts and twinkling lights. But would it fly?

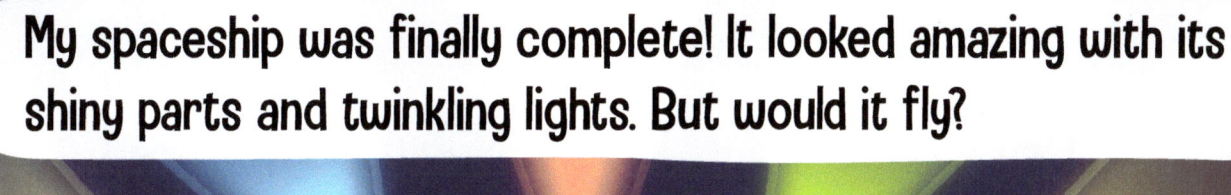

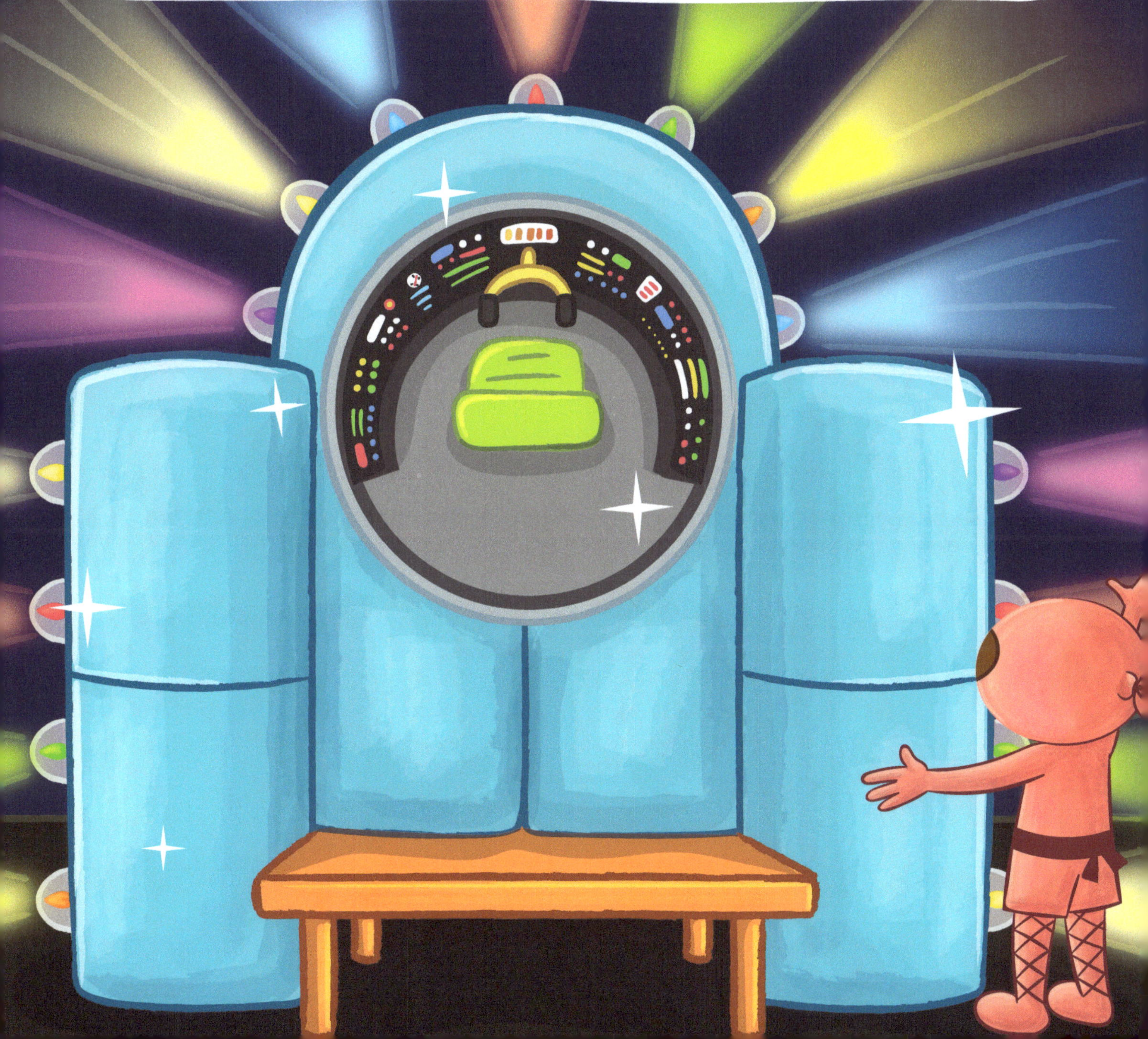

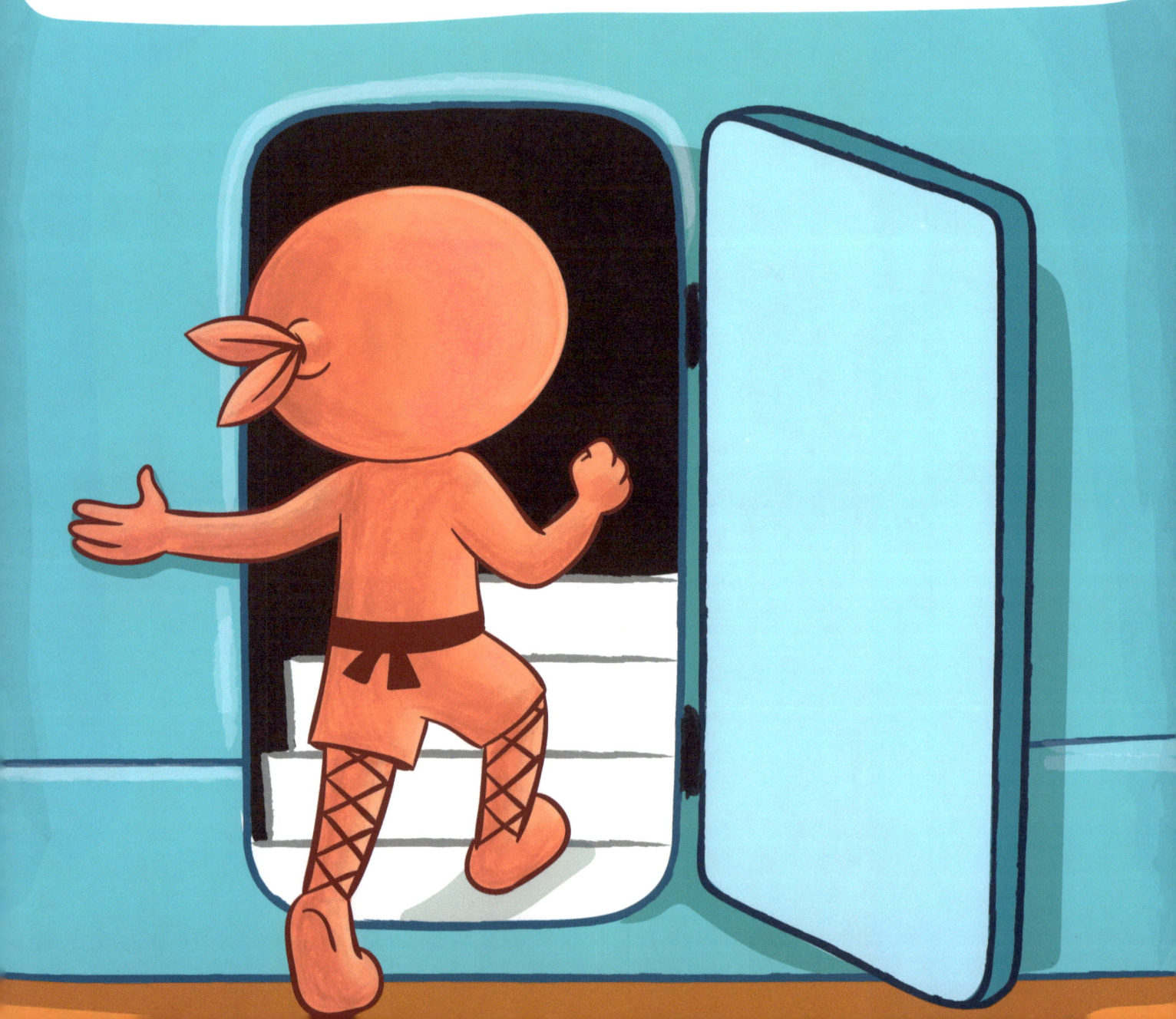

I climbed aboard, closed my eyes, and imagined soaring through galaxies. I whispered, "3, 2, 1... Blast off!" And guess what?

Zoom! My spaceship soared high into the sky. I felt like a real astronaut exploring the universe!

As I flew past planets and stars, I realized being a visionary meant believing in my dreams and making them real.

Now, I use what I've learned to help others and make the world brighter. I may be young, but I am a visionary!

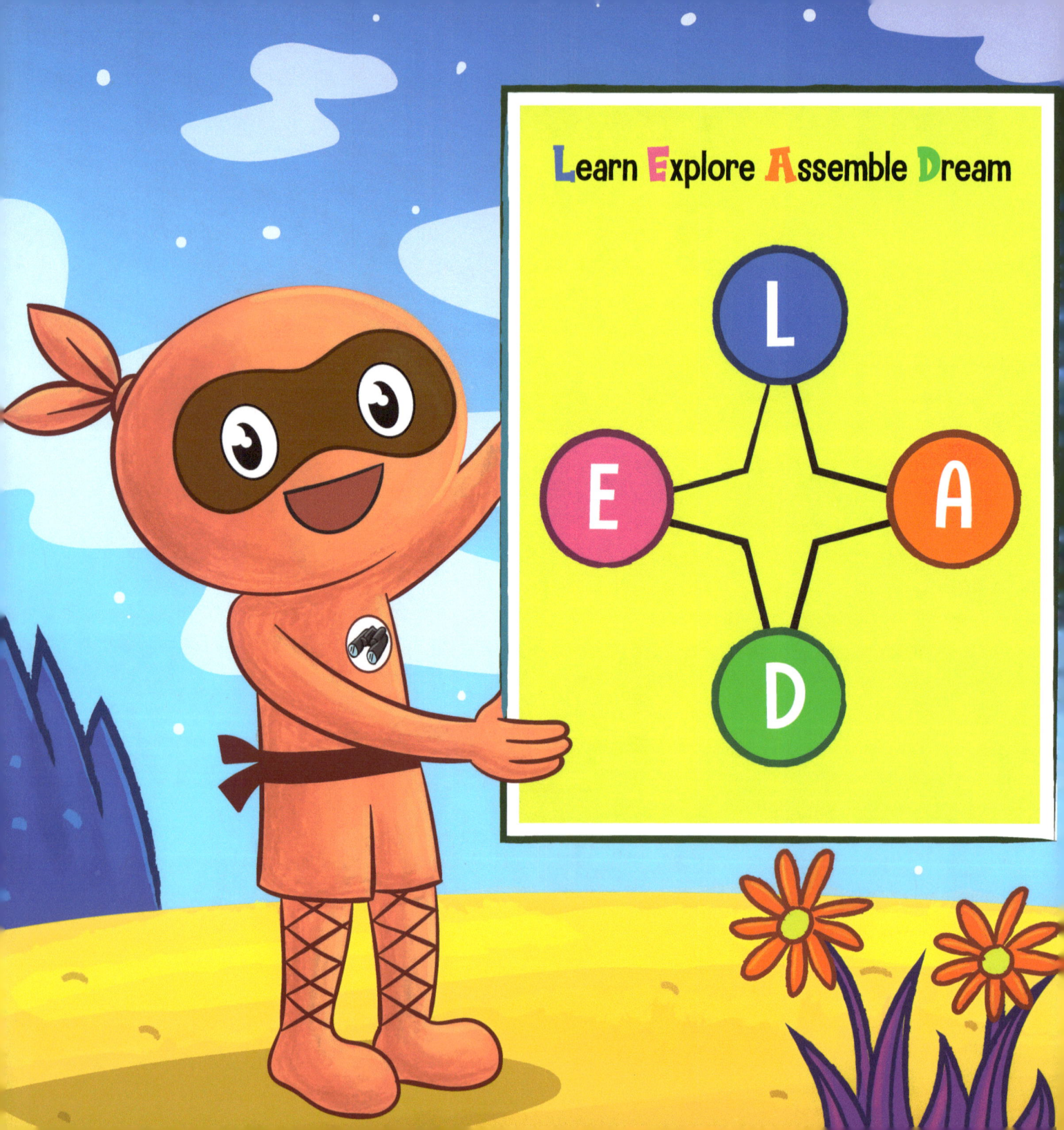

Remembering L.E.A.D. could be your secret weapon in becoming the next visionary.

Learn, Explore, Assemble, and Dream.

Believe in your dreams, and you'll do amazing things.

Continue the learning with the Visionary Ninja lesson plans which include superpower skills practice, STEM activity, craft, and more! Visit NinjaLifeHacks.tv

 @marynhin @officialninjalifehacks
#NinjaLifeHacks

 Ninja Life Hacks

 Mary Nhin   Ninja Life Hacks

 @officialninjalifehacks

www.ingramcontent.com/pod-product-compliance
Lightning Source LLC
Chambersburg PA
CBHW041521070526
44585CB00002B/35